# ARROWVILLE

Story & Pictures By Geefwee Boedoe

LAURA GERINGER BOOKS

*An Imprint of* HarperCollins *Publishers*

Beyond the Arrow Mountains, where winds blow bitter chill, across the Arrow Ocean lies a town called Arrowville.

Arrowville was never slow—a constant go, go, go!
In a manic panic people hustled to and fro.
Every pointed person had a pointed point of view,
and every point in Arrowville was always just askew.

Once a year at school there came
a special prize event,
a competition solely
for the sake of argument.
All pupils practiced arguing
at lunch and recess too—
all except for Barb, that is,
who dreamily withdrew.

The quarrel contest started—the time was five to three—
but ended most abruptly when Barb said, "I agree."

Barb was sent directly home in horrible disgrace
with a note of reprimand—a frown upon her face.

Barb's father was the mayor. "Now get it though your head.
You can't keep on agreeing. You must dispute instead.
You must rebuke, refute, retort. That's the proper way.
Don't use words like 'I agree,' 'Yes,' or 'That's OK.'"

That night Barb felt atrocious
and wrote a good-bye letter,
then vanished in the moonlight
with her backpack and a sweater.

Morning came with warnings blaring:

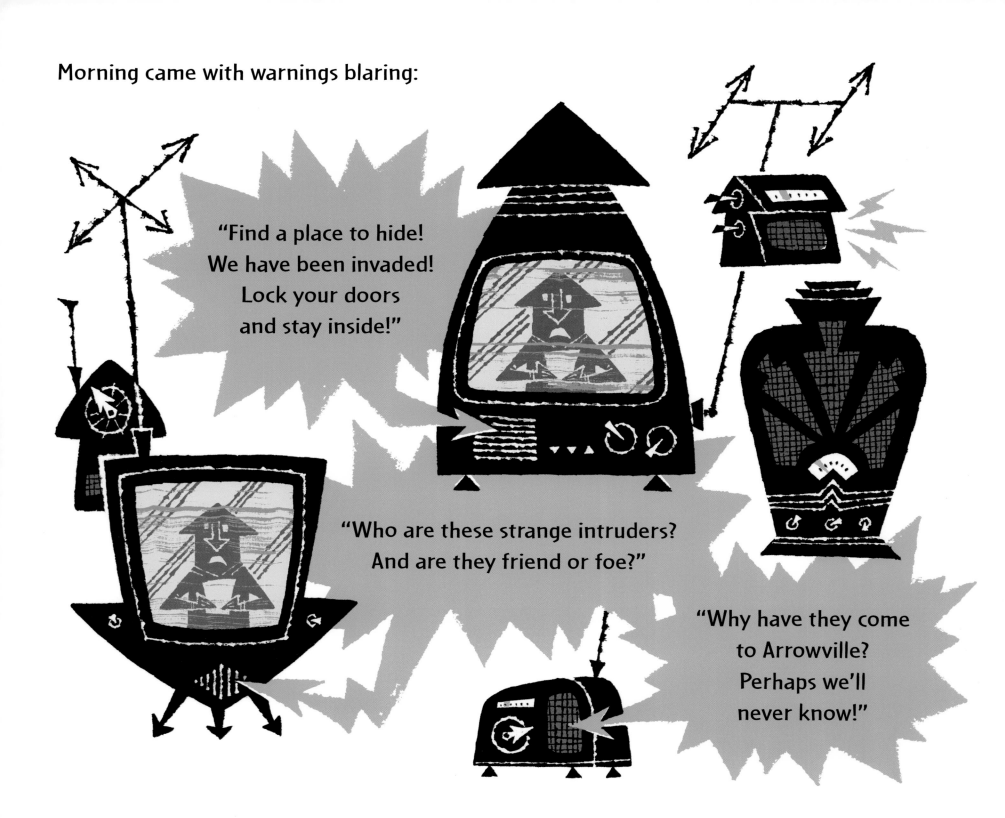

"Find a place to hide!
We have been invaded!
Lock your doors
and stay inside!"

"Who are these strange intruders?
And are they friend or foe?"

"Why have they come
to Arrowville?
Perhaps we'll
never know!"

Barb's parents ran to tell her in a frenzied frantic fright,
but found her room quite empty—no letter was in sight.
They thought the worst. They didn't know that Barb had run away.
"The strangers! She's been kidnaped!" they both shouted in dismay.

The strangers were vacationing, or that was their intent.
But one wrong turn and they arrived in town by accident.
Mr. Target mumbled with his map turned upside down,
while Mrs. Target whispered, "There's not a soul in town."

"This must be a ghost town," their son, Bullseye, said with zeal.
It seemed a great vacation spot with genuine appeal.
"Oh! What fun!" they all three cheered. "Let's stay here for the day."
(While filled with curiosity, Barb watched from far away.)

They stopped at the museum, jam-packed with things to see,
with furniture and fashions documenting history.
Bullseye liked the ancient bones of creatures most colossal
and imitated every face he saw upon each fossil.
Antique clocks and vintage socks all perfectly pristine,
and Mrs. Target wondered how this ghost town stayed so clean.

Their next stop was the noisiest. It was the Arrow zoo,
with shrieking birds and monkeys and a thumping kangaroo.
The tiger's roar was loud indeed, but loudest of the bunch
was Bullseye's stomach growling when it was time for lunch.

They found a perfect picnic park and ate their ideal meal:
peanut butter, sassafras, and candied orange peel.
While the Targets peacefully enjoyed the food and weather,
down at City Hall the Arrow Council came together.

No one knew just what to do
about these odd new strangers,
and so they clamored on and on
about potential dangers.
The Mayor rushed into the room.
"They've got my little girl!"
"To the rescue! Quick!" they gasped,
then raced off in a whirl.

After lunch the Targets played a friendly game of catch,
until their ball crashed through a bush, finishing their match.

"YEOW!" the bush wailed violently, and shook from side to side.
"A haunted shrub!" the Targets gasped with eyes popped open wide.
But girl, not ghost, crawled from the shrub. The Targets were surprised,
then offered Barb a lollypop as they apologized.

"What's a lollypop?" Barb asked. "A toy or giant pill?"
For such a treat did not exist in all of Arrowville.
"It's candy, and we make them from our family recipe."
The Targets spoke together—in three-part harmony.

Just then the frenzied Arrow mob came storming into sight.
"We want the girl," the mob yelled out, "and we're prepared to fight!"
Barb and the Targets were perplexed and also mortified.
With scurry, scuttle, scampering they found a place to hide.

"The town has gone completely mad." Barb shook her head, aghast.
"We can't hide here forever. We've got to leave—and fast!"
So quickly they devised a plan to make their grand escape
with tarp and twine and odds and ends and lots of masking tape.

Carefully they crept away, concealed by their disguise,
passing crowds on every street, avoiding watchful eyes.

Then a snag revealed their ploy.
"It's time to try plan B!"

On a makeshift cart they sped—
their final hope to flee.

A zooming fuming fever fit—
a chasing racing roar!
All Arrowville came closing in!
Now what would be in store?

The whole town yelled, "Give us the girl!"
The warning pierced the air.
The Targets screamed, "Don't hurt the girl!
Don't harm a single hair!"
Arrowville was clouded
with confusion and dismay.
The Targets had not kidnaped her—
Barb had run away!
Barb then told her story
from beginning to the end—
of how she met the Targets
and became their new-found friend.
Silence fell upon the crowd—
they knew that they'd been wrong.
But from the Targets came a sound,
growing clear and strong.

This whole absurd confusion burst the Targets into laughter,
which quickly spread into the crowd immediately after.

The Targets passed out lollypops,
an added bonus treat,
and all who gave a lick declared,
"This taste cannot be beat."

"I think our town should make amends
and build a nice retreat—
a place just for the Targets.
A place that's fine and sweet.
The Targets then could visit us
at any time of year.
What do you say, good people?"
the Mayor spoke with cheer.
Then to Barb's amazement,
to her surprise and glee,
all of Arrowville together shouted . . .

So every year to Arrowville the Targets came to visit
and stayed at their vacation house, which they thought quite exquisite.
Arrowville was much the same and always on the go,
with hustle, bustle, arguing, and racing to and fro.
But all of Arrowville agreed—east, west, and up and down,
that smack-dab in the middle was the sweetest spot in town. . . .

*For Coralie*

Arrowville
Copyright © 2004 by Geefwee Boedoe
Manufactured in China by South China Printing Company Ltd.
All rights reserved.
www.harperchildrens.com

Library of Congress Cataloging-in-Publication Data
Boedoe, Geefwee.
  Arrowville / Story & pictures by Geefwee Boedoe.— 1st ed.
    p.   cm.
  Summary: When the Target family travels through Arrowville, the people there initially
mistake them for enemies.
  ISBN 0-06-055598-X — ISBN 0-06-055599-8 (lib. bdg.)
  [1. Prejudices—Fiction.  2. Stories in rhyme—Fiction.]  I. Title.
PZ8.3.B59952Ar 2004
[E]—dc21                                                                    2003011289
                                                                                  CIP
                                                                                   AC

Typography by Alicia Mikles
1 2 3 4 5 6 7 8 9 10
❖
First Edition